MINOTAUR'S MUSE

ARLA JONES

Illustrations by Lauren Hanson

Edited by Kate Seger

This has also been published as a serial fiction on Kindle Vella.

1st Edition 2023

ACKNOWLEDGEMENTS

Thank you, Kate Seger, for your detailed editing, and Lauren, the header is perfect for this story.

CONTENTS

CHAPTER 1

KING MINOS GIVES
AN ASSIGNMENT

King Minos sat on his throne wearing his indigo-blue, silver-embroidered tunic and a midnight-blue cloak attached to a large golden brooch. He squeezed his eyes shut, berating himself for being gullible.

Today, he didn't want to meet any of his subjects or settle any arguments over land or crops. He couldn't care less if someone's sheep had been stolen or if there was a dispute about who owned the land by the river bend.

King Minos sighed. He leaned his head on his hand and looked distraught. Something was wrong with his wife. She was no longer interested in sharing their bed. She claimed to have headaches and be tired.

King Minos was a sturdy, haughty man with curly hair, and he wore a jewel-decorated golden diadem.

He was not used to being turned down or lied to, but he was sure his wife, Queen Pasiphaë, had been untruthful to him for the past few days. He had awoken later that night and saw her rushing through the garden in her white tunic, her long reddish hair flowing on her back and shoulders. She had snuck out after she had denied him entrance to her bedroom. Why? King Minos shook his head in disbelief. Leaving the castle in a hurry soon afterward was not like her, and King Minos wanted to find out what was going on.

He called on his trusted advisor, Leon, to meet him. When Leon arrived, the king commanded, "Find out what Queen Pasiphaë's secret is. I want to know everything."

Leon had a fox-like face and thinning hair down to his shoulders. He was smart, calculating, and ready to serve.

He knew he would be rewarded heftily if he discovered the truth. He bowed almost to the floor level and said, "I will do as you wish, my lord king." And he exited the throne room, leaving King Minos in a foul mood. A skinny man with quick eyes and long limbs, he took long strides as he walked past the marble statues and smooth columns of the long halls leading to the castle's front door.

Leon knew his worth well. His investigative skills were excellent; thus, King Minos had used his services many times before. He had always been loyal and resourceful, and the king trusted him to bring him news and reports of his enemies. This time though, he had to spy on the queen. When he walked out of the castle, he decided to wait until nighttime to find out where the queen was visiting without telling the king. *It must be a secret because why else would she sneak out without a word,* Leon thought. He was not liked among the king's advisors and soldiers because they never knew if he was spying on them or badmouthing them to the king. Leon had earned the king's trust, but at the same time, he had gained the distrust of the other advisors and officers. He had no friends. No one liked him. No one trusted him.

Leon walked through the garden, the same path the queen had taken the previous night, and then sat down on one of the benches. This would be a good place to wait, he thought. He glanced at the sky. *It will be clear tonight. Easy to see anyone moving in the moonlight,* he thought. The sun would set in a few hours. He'd still had time. He didn't believe the queen would leave earlier. She'd wait for the darkness of the night.

CHAPTER 2

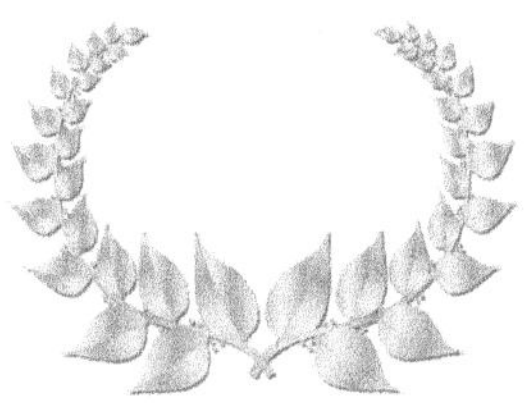

QUEEN PASIPHAË'S SECRET

Leon waited for hours in the garden. He was like a still statue sitting on the bench, watching the shadows grow longer as time passed.

The sky was painted red, purple, yellow, and orange as the sun gradually vanished on the horizon, leaving the night sky dark except for bright stars and a full moon.

Leon stirred and sat straight. He got up and moved into the shadow of the nearby tree so that he would not be visible. Soon, the queen would arrive. He was sure of it. Queen Pasiphaë would not wait past midnight. The previous night she had left shortly after dinner. He didn't believe the queen would change her plans tonight, either.

Thanks to the gods, he didn't have to wait more hours. Leon saw a form of a woman appearing from the castle and running through the garden, heading toward his position. He withdrew himself from the view of the path and kept his eyes on the woman. She had pulled her scarf over her head, but Leon recognized her as the queen. She didn't look around. The thought that she could be spied on and followed had not even crossed her mind. She walked past the bench where Leon had sat earlier that evening and ran toward the small gate that led out of the castle's garden and to a side alley.

Leon followed her.

She walked along the alley, turned the corner, and headed toward the harbor and the ships.

Why is she going there? Leon wondered but kept his pace and ensured she didn't notice him following her. The queen never looked back. She had no idea that her husband was suspicious. *Good, that makes my job easier,* Leon thought.

When they reached the harbor, Leon stopped by the last building and carefully peaked around the corner. He saw the queen running to the arms of a handsome young soldier, hugging, and kissing him.

The two lovers only saw each other. After their steamy embrace, they walked to the beach and strolled on the sand hand in hand until they were not visible from the ships or the road around the island.

Leon had walked on the roadside, keeping an eye on them, but when they finally sat down, Leon decided to find out who this man was. He knew nothing about him except the ship where he came from, so he returned to the harbor and looked around. He recognized the ship, which was called Persiphone. It was King Midas's ship made for trade and war.

Leon walked along the pier, and when he saw another soldier, he called, "Hello, can you help me?"

The soldier stopped and looked at Leon. "Perhaps. What do you want?"

Leon walked closer. Now, he had to be careful not to give up his identity and that of whom he was following.

"Good evening, sir. I was supposed to meet a friend of a friend here by the pier. Did you see another soldier waiting here a while ago?"

"Yes, I did. Christos stayed behind for quite a while and waited for someone. You just missed him. He left a couple of minutes ago." The man looked at him, adding, "He met a woman, though. I don't think that's the man you were looking for, is he?"

Leon shook his head. "No, I don't think he's the one. I was going to meet a soldier who could help me to go to Corinth."

"No, I don't think I can help you with that. I didn't see anyone else here tonight," the soldier replied.

"Thank you for your help," Leon said and walked away. He knew the name of the queen's lover: Christos.

CHAPTER 3

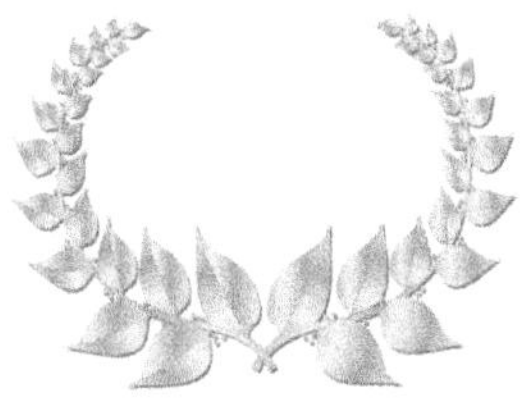

QUEEN PASIPHAË AND CHRISTOS

Christos lay next to Pasiphaë on the cooling sand and kissed her on the forehead. "My love, my heart, you are so beautiful," he said adoringly.

His fighting tunic smelled like sweat and dirt as he had practiced sword fighting with his fellow soldiers all afternoon. A week ago, their ship had returned from Rhodos, where they had fought the rogue pirates that sometimes preyed on the harbors for traders. His long golden locks reached his shoulders. His broad shoulders revealed well-trained muscles, and his biceps were thick like logs.

Pasiphaë smiled and turned her face toward the sea. The waves rolled to the shore at a steady pace. "My love, you have my heart. I wish I could be with you forever."

Christos looked thoughtful. "You know your husband will never let you go. You are his possession, his queen."

Pasiphaë looked down, and her face turned dark. "I know that. I fear what he will do if he ever finds out about us."

"Let us pray to the gods that he never discovers our secret. Our love is pure and does not need to be sullied in public or threatened by the king." Christos sounded assured when he said that. He touched Pasiphaë's cheek, grabbed her chin, and kissed her fiercely. Pasiphaë leaned closer to him, her arms around his neck, and they stayed like that for a long time.

"When do you have to leave?" Pasiphaë asked when they withdrew from each other's arms.

"Soon. The ship is ready to go, and we'll wait for the king's orders on where to head next time. The captain will go to see the king, and he should get his orders tomorrow,"

Christos replied, caressing Pasiphaë's long hair with his hand.

"I wish you didn't have to go so soon. You just got back," Pasiphaë replied. "Could you stay behind?"

"No, I can't. I'm a soldier in the king's army. I can't choose when or where to go," he replied.

The queen sighed. "I should return to the palace before anyone notices I'm gone. I don't want to explain where I was or why," she said, sitting up.

Christos pulled her back. "Just a little while longer," he whispered to her ear, kissed her passionately on the lips, then moved his hot lips along his white neck to her shoulder and then down to her breasts. Pasiphaë inhaled quickly as Christos's lips reached her breast. She grabbed him tight and let him continue for a while. She felt his hard body pressing hers.

Gently, she pushed him away. "We can't. What if someone sees us here?"

Christos took deep breaths to calm himself. He stood up and pulled her up next to him. "Not today, but someday, I swear, you'll be mine." Kissing her one more time, Christos took her hand, and they started walking away back to the harbor. The waves lapped the shoreline with a faint calming sound.

Pasiphaë inhaled the sweet scent of pink oleanders blooming along the roadside. Christos picked one pink flower and put it behind her ear. "A flower for my beauty."

Pasiphaë smiled, and her eyes sparkled with happiness. These moments with Christos were the reason she could endure the dull life of the palace with the man he didn't love or care for. Her marriage to King Minos had been arranged, and she had never been asked what she wanted or whom she wished to marry.

When they reached the pier, Christos reluctantly pulled his hand from hers, and she slunk into the shadows heading back to her luxurious prison, the palace.

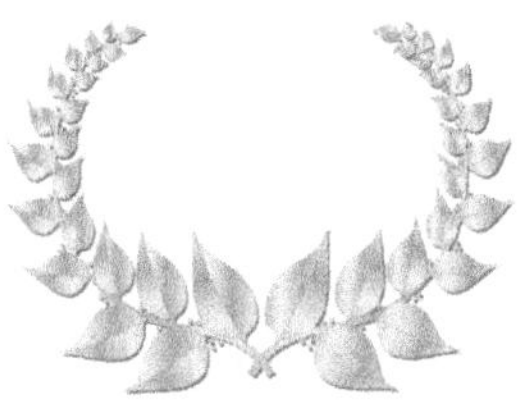

CHAPTER 4

KING MINOS AND QUEEN PASIPHAË

The next day, Leon went to the soldiers' quarters to find out more about Christos as he had only his name and knew nothing else about him yet. King Minos would want to learn more about this man who had taken the queen's heart.

Leon asked around about who this strapping young soldier Christos was. He finally found out that he was one of the most successful fighters in the king's army. He was well-liked among men and women. He had no trouble finding a companion if he needed one. However, his colleagues revealed to Leon that Christos had not gone out with them to drink after work for some time now. He had been distracted as if something weighed on his mind heavily.

While Leon was gathering more information, Queen Pasiphaë met King Minos at breakfast, and they sat there together, not exchanging any words, while the servants brought them fruits and porridge with red wine and water to drink. King Minos looked pensive as he ate, leaving the breakfast room soon after he had finished his meal.

Queen Pasiphaë glanced curiously after him as he had said hardly any word to her all morning. Something was wrong, she was sure, but she had no idea what. *Perhaps, the king was only angry and disappointed because I didn't let him into my bedroom the last two nights,* she thought, furrowing her brows. *I must be careful. I don't want him to get angry. I've seen his rage and what he can do. He's not kind and kills all his opponents. He is not afraid of torturing enemies or leaving them crippled or half-dead. I don't wish to be his enemy,* Pasiphaë thought. She brushed her hands on the hem of her white tunic, stood up, walked to the tall window, and glanced outside.

It was a beautiful morning with a bright blue sky, no clouds, and the sea gleamed greenish-blue. The waves were rolling gently to the shore. She loved the view from the palace as it was built in a higher place with a clear view of the sea. When Christos had been traveling with the ship to Rhodes, she had often stood here wondering if she would see his vessel arriving at Crete's harbor soon. And how she would run down to the pier, wrap her arms around him, and kiss him hard. Pasiphaë wished she wouldn't have to worry about her husband, the king, but she knew she could never escape her prison. She would be married to the king as long as she lived.

Sighing, she turned away from the window. Now, she would have to pretend to be a good queen and find something to do in the palace while waiting for the evening and meeting Christos again.

As a queen, she was merely a trophy, an object of King Minos's desire used to ensure the continuation of his family line. She wished to be more to him and this kingdom when she married. King Minos, however, didn't want to give her any more power or a greater role in the palace. She wasn't stupid. She knew she could advise on political and social topics. She understood that life on this island was mostly blessed because the rivers provided fertile soil, and the subjects could grow various vegetables and fruits there. They had no frost, and the storms usually only harmed the fishermen. So, she believed she could have been more helpful to this island than being just a queen to serve at the king's pleasure.

She could have helped the women on this island by educating them about the different possibilities in trade and skilled craftwork instead of just staying at home. She had also considered offering a yearly fund for the widows after they had lost their husbands, and were left alone with no one to take care of the family. She had seen that sad story around the island, and she believed that the kingdom could benefit if they helped the suffering families.

CHAPTER 5

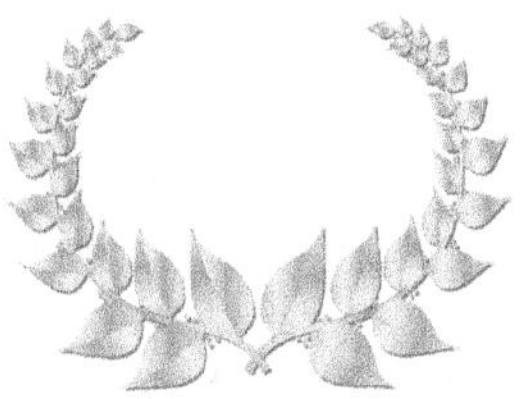

LEON

He pushed open the door that led to the soldier's quarters in the palace. It was near the front gate in case enemies tried to attack. He looked around to find the other soldiers and their captain to ask more about Christos. Then he located his captain and asked more about the young man. After half an hour's discussion with the captain and the other soldier, who was Christos's close friend, Leon had all the information he needed for the king.

Leon had explained to Captain Theo and Christos's best friend Mikhalis that the king was planning a new secret mission and needed trustworthy soldiers. They were considered for this task. Of course, both men freely told him everything they knew about Christos and how brave and skillful he was. Besides, they all knew that if the king was going to send Christos for a secret mission, the whole ship crew would go with him. Thus, it would be better if they answered truthfully and even praised the young man in question.

Leon left the soldiers' quarters when he got all he needed. However, he warned the captain and Mikhalis not to tell Christos anything about this because they would not want to upset the king or let enemy spies know about the king's task beforehand.

Leon rubbed his hands together as he had now all he needed. His skinny figure strolled inside the palace and headed toward the throne room. He expected to find King Minos there.

He slowed his pace as he considered what he had to tell the king. His queen cheated him with an ordinary soldier who was not even an officer or an aristocrat. They had shown their love in plain sight, although it had been dark and nighttime. No one could say they were hiding because Leon had seen with his eyes that they kissed and hugged on the public beach.

He knew King Minos's temper. He could be vicious and unforgiven. Leon stopped by the window and stared outside. He had to consider the best way to present this affair to him without risking his neck. He knew that King Minos did not like the bearers of bad news. Leon was worried about his wrath and that the king would target him too.

He sighed. Better go now and tell the king what he had found out and try to present the topic lightly. He wasn't sure if he could do that, but he would try it.

Thus, Leon continued his walk along the hallway toward the throne room. He glanced inside. The king was sitting on his throne and listening to some complaints of his subjects, looking distracted and irritated. When Leon stepped inside, King Minos turned his eyes toward him with a question, and when Leon nodded, the king ordered the room to be emptied immediately.

Leon swallowed hard. Now, he'd have to present the facts. He went to the throne and said, "My king, I have found out what you asked me to do."

King Minos nodded. "Tell me." His eyes burned as he looked into Leon's eyes.

Leon shivered. "The queen snuck out to meet a man. It seems they met some months ago."

"Who is this man?" King Minos asked with a calm voice. His eyes were hard like stone, and Leon was sure the king was furious but hiding his true feelings.

"Christos. A soldier who recently returned from Rhodes." Leon stood still, looking at the king.

King Minos asked, "Is my wife in love with this man?" Now, this was the question Leon had considered how to answer.

Leon decided to tell the king what he saw. "The queen and this man seemed to be very friendly, even amorous."

King Minos slammed his fist on the throne's armrest. "Tell me exactly what you saw!" King Minos's eyes flashed in anger.

"The couple went to the beach, where they stayed for hours kissing and hugging," Leon replied truthfully.

"Are they lovers?" King Minos asked with a low tone, more threatening than his raised voice a moment ago.

"I don't know that, but they seemed to know each other well, and the queen seemed to enjoy this soldier's embrace and kisses." Leon waited for the king's reply.

"I will ask you not to tell anyone anything about this." King Minos looked pensive and said, "Ask the ship's captain to see me. I have a special task for him. He needs to leave immediately with all his men."

"All of them?" Leon repeated.

"Yes, all of them." King Minos stared at Leon for a moment and added, "And you will go with them to make sure they will follow my orders to the tiniest detail."

"Me? With the ship?" Leon looked puzzled. This was not what he had expected.

"Yes, I need to have my loyal servant on the ship to make sure the captain does as I order. Now, go and fetch this captain for me. I have to give him detailed instructions for his next trip." King Minos leaned back on his throne. His face was unemotional but calculative. He had decided what to do with the lover boy.

Leon was another matter. King Minos didn't want anyone who knew about his queen's indiscretion to be alive and here on this island... If she had children then there would always be rumors about who was the real father, and he wanted none of that. He wanted to keep his own family's reputation clean, and that meant Leon was doomed when he witnessed the love affair. King Minos was sad when he wrote his sentence in the letter, but he had no choice. Two men would enter the island, and only one would return, and it would not be Leon.

Confused, Leon bowed and walked away. Had he succeeded or failed? He wasn't sure. This trip might be a good sign. If the king trusted him and wanted him to supervise the journey and the captain's orders. However, it could be just the opposite too. If the king wanted to get rid of him, the open sea would be a perfect place to throw him overboard. He had to be very careful and watch his back from now on.

Worried, Leon returned to the soldiers' quarters, found the captain he had spoken with a while ago, asked him to see the king, and told him that the next voyage across the sea would start today.

CHAPTER 6

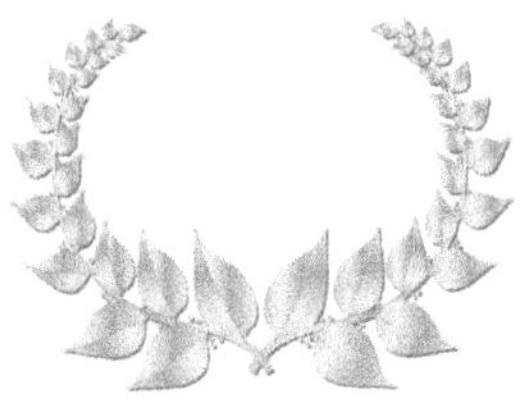

KING MINOS AND
CAPTAIN THEO

While King Minos waited for the captain to come to see him, he went to his treasure chamber and brought out a jewelry box filled with coins, pearls, and jewels.

Today King Minos looked quite dashing with his dark blue tunic and dark red silk cape fastened at the shoulder by a golden brooch shaped like a curling snake with a charging bull embroidered on it. The bull was his symbol since his coronation when Poseidon, the god of the sea and storm, presented him with a white bull.

He sat by the table, wrote a note on parchment paper, pressed his sigil on the bottom of the page, rolled the letter to a scroll, and tied a ribbon around it.

The sound of footsteps approaching alerted the king, and he returned to his throne, leaving the jewelry box and the scroll on the table.

Captain Theo wore a grey tunic with a black cloak, with a sword and dagger on his belt. He had dark hair and a short beard like many islanders. He kneeled in front of the throne, keeping his eyes cast down. "My king."

"Stand up. I have a mission for you," King Minos said curtly. "Take the box and the scroll with you. You will go to Circe's Island."

"Circe? The witch's island! But I've heard rumors that she is an incredibly skilled and evil enchantress. I've heard that the ships that go there don't return, and the crew have vanished or even worse," Captain Theo protested.

"Just rumors. I have an offer for her in exchange for her services. The jewelry box is her payment for the service.

The scroll is for her to read. Only her." King Minos stared at the captain, who nodded reluctantly.

"Yes, my king," Captain Theo replied.

"I have more instructions for you. Only Leon and Christos can go to the shore when you arrive at the shores of the sorceress's island. No one else will follow them. They will go to meet Circe alone. They will take this scroll and the jewelry box to her. She will find her instructions on the scroll I wrote." King Minos kept his eyes steady on Captain Theo. He saw Theo furrow his brows.

Theo didn't object to the king but said, "Yes, my king. I will follow your orders. We will leave today as soon as the ship is ready."

"That's all. You may prepare your ship and crew for the journey." King Minos waved his hand, gesturing that the captain was allowed to leave his presence. The captain bowed and marched out of the throne room with the jewelry box and the scroll.

He had not asked why Leon and Christos should go to meet Circe, the sorceress. It was not his business to know. *The scroll must have the answers, and Circe will do as the king had asked,* Captain Theo thought as he walked out of the palace.

The sky was clear as the captain walked down the hill from the palace to the harbor. Flowering bushes and trees filled the roadside.

The harbor was filled with ships, but only Captain Theo's had sails full and the crew buzzing around carrying food and water from the shore into the ship's galley for the coming journey.

Captain Theo's ship was a trireme, a warship made of cypress inside and the hull made of oak. It had twenty-five oars on each side. The trireme had a bronze-sheathed battering ram, the shape of an ox's head, affixed to the prow used to sink enemy ships. Because the ship was built for combat, the storage area was reserved for extra oars, and only the minimum space was left for food and water. The captain wasn't concerned about that because the Mediterranean Sea was peppered with other islands. Usually, it was easy to gather more food and fresh water on the way to the destination. This time though, they were not headed for battle, so he ordered them to bring in more food and water and leave extra oars behind. He didn't expect any fights on this trip.

Later that afternoon, the ship sailed away from Crete with Leon and Christos.

Leon was concerned about why he had to be on this ship. When they were further away from Crete, he asked the captain, "Do you know why King Minos insisted that I go on this journey with you?" He tried to avoid looking concerned, but a tick under his right eye gave away his nervousness.

Captain Theo turned to face him, his cloak billowing behind him in the wind. "I was told to take this ship to Circe's Island, and there, you will accompany Christos to meet the sorceress. King Minos handed me a handwritten scroll that you will give to the sorceress and a jewelry box as a present to Circe. That's all I know."

Leon inhaled deeply and let it out slowly. That didn't sound so worrying. Perhaps King Minos wanted him to make sure Christos really went ashore and saw the witch and didn't run away. *That must be it,* he thought. He felt much better after coming to that conclusion. *I can consider this trip a reward for my loyalty,* Leon thought, facing the horizon and enjoying the strong wind.

CHAPTER 7

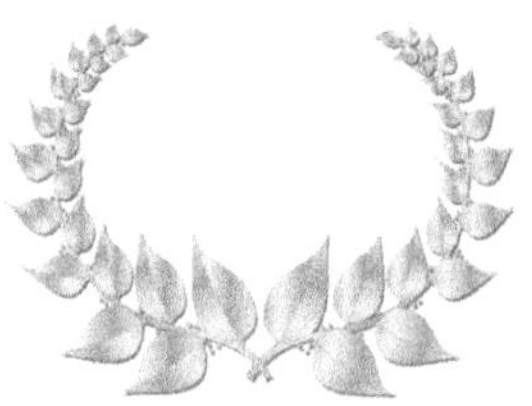

CIRCE'S ISLAND

While many small islands were stony and scarce of vegetation, Circe's Island was lush with cypress trees, bushes, and ground vegetation. It lay far to the north of Crete, and the captain had never traveled that distance before. He had avoided the cursed place based on the rumors he had heard of the sorceress Circe.

As they approached the island, Captain Theo ordered the crew to reduce speed and lowered the sails. They stopped further from the shoreline so the ship would not crash into any underlying rocks.

The water looked clear, and they could see to the bottom of the sea. The captain pointed out some weird-looking fish and large sea snakes that swam away from the ship. "I've never seen anything like those before, and I've visited most of the islands in the Mediterranean."

"Perhaps those creatures were enchanted," Leon suggested. "This island is the sorceress's island. She is known for her evil skills."

As the ship got ready to lower a small boat for Christos and Leon, they saw a flock of multicolored birds flying through the forest. "They look beautiful," Christos said, awed.

"They might be Circe's handiwork, too," Captain Theo said. "Be careful when you go to see her." He handed the scroll to Leon and the jewelry box to Christos. "Have a safe trip to her island and back. We'll wait for your return here."

Christos and Leon left the ship, not really knowing what to expect. They only knew the king's orders, and they obeyed them. Christos lowered the expensive box on the bottom of the small boat, then took the oars and rowed to the shore. Leon and Christos pulled the boat up so it would not float away with the high tide. As they were doing that, they heard the clippety-clop sounds of hooves behind them, and they looked up. A tribe of white, black, and brown goats approached them, bleating as if they were afraid of something. They surrounded the two men and kept pushing them back toward their small boat.

"What is this all about?" Leon asked, puzzled. "It's like these goats want us to leave this island."

"It must be a sorceress's trickery." Christos pushed the nearest goat away gently. The others bleated around the two men, but they did not understand why the goats were acting this way, driving them and trying to stop them from going past. "Sorry goats, but you've got to let us pass. We have a business to tend to," Christos said, and the goats finally let them move forward. They stayed by the small boat staring after the two men as if they were doomed.

Leon glanced back at the goats. They were gathered around the boat staring at them and bleating sadly. "Those goats act so humanly. I wish I knew what they wanted from us."

"We can't stay and wonder what the goats are doing. We need to find the sorceress and give her the jewelry box and the scroll and then get out of this enchanted island," Christos replied, marching upwards and heading to the forest. Leon followed him, but he still had doubts about this island and their mission there.

A river crossed the forest like a blue snake slithering among the trees. The men followed the river upwards until they saw the forest's edge ahead.

The large colorful birds they had seen from the ship attacked the men suddenly. Like a large flock of feathers, sharp claws, and beaks, the birds flew downward, tried to hit the men, then swooped upward again. Christos and Leon cursed and ran faster until they reached the last trees, and as suddenly as the flock of birds had appeared, they disappeared. It was as if they could not go past the tree line

.

Both Christos and Leon sighed and slowed their pace to a normal walk again. "This island is cursed. No wonder no one wants to come here," Christos muttered.

Leon decided this was a perfect time to ask Christos about this mission. "Have you thought at all about why you were chosen for this task?"

Christos glanced at his companion. "King Minos orders his soldiers to go where he needs us to go. I obey. I don't ask questions."

Ah, if only it was that simple, Leon thought. This man had no idea that his love affair with the queen was now out in the open and that the king knew about him. Poor guy. *When he returns to Crete, King Minos will probably imprison him or kill him. I don't believe he has a future on that island,* Leon thought grimly. He knew how ruthless King Minos was to his enemies, and he was sure that the king would not be kind or forgiven to his wife's lover.

They marched through high grass, and after another ten minutes of walking, they saw what looked like pens for pigs, geese, and chickens. Behind the pens was a palace of yellow stone with pillars in front. "I think we found where Circe lives," Leon said, nodding toward the structure. They passed a herb and flower garden with beautiful white, red, and blue flowers and headed to the front door.

A servant appeared in the doorway. He was half human and half goat. He blew a trumpet announcing the visitors.

Both Christos and Leon stared at the man. His upper body was human, with a handsome young male face and golden hair, whereas his legs were furry goat legs. "I've never seen anything like that," Leon muttered as they slowed their pace and approached the servant.

The servant said, "This way, please. My lady is waiting for you. She saw your ship arrive at the shore a while ago." He gestured to a large hallway and walked ahead of them, his hooves making clip-clop sounds on the white marble floor.

The hallway had natural-looking statues of men in different positions, but what was most curious was that their faces looked horrified. Christos and Leon slowed and stared at each one of the statues. Some were made of gold, some silver or bronze. "Why do all of these statues look scared or distraught?" Christos asked.

The servant boy heard and replied, "Because they were.. All of these statues were men like you or me before they met Circe."

Christos and Leon glanced at each other. At that moment, when they saw the statues, they realized that this mission was a trap. They should never have come to this island.

CHAPTER 8

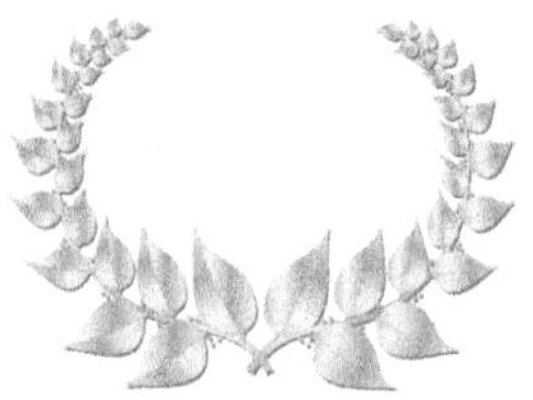

CIRCE

The servant stopped by a large dining room and said, "Please, go in. My lady is waiting for you there." He stayed behind as both Leon and Christos stepped forward.

They were curious, but the first thing they saw was the dinner table in the middle of the room with various meat, vegetables, berries, and fruits. A golden decorative fountain statue presenting a dolphin was set in the middle of the dinner table, and instead of water, red wine ran down from its mouth.

The dishes looked so delicious that the men just stared at them and then took a few steps toward the table.

"Please, sit down and eat. You have all the time in the world," a strange singsong voice said from the shadows of the room, and as they tried to see who had spoken to them, a beautiful woman stepped forward from the darkness.

Her long stunning raven hair spilled down her back. She stared at them with piercing blue eyes, and her plump lips curved into a smile. Her gown was lilac with a heavy golden belt and necklaces. She was a vision of beauty.

Christos quickly dusted his hands over his tunic before straightening his back. He saluted. "Circe, I assume? I have a scroll and a jewelry box from our king Minos from Crete. He has a request for you, and the payment is in this box."

She halted mid-stride as their gazes met. Her eyes wandered from his handsome face to his strong arms and then his muscular body, and her lips moved silently for a second or two as if casting a spell.

When she came closer, Leon handed her the scroll King Minos had written, and Christos gave her the jewelry box. Both men then stood there waiting for her to read it.

"Please, eat and rest. I'm going to read the scroll now," Circe said, moving to the next chair and sitting down.

The men sat down by the table and started eating. They were hungry.

Meanwhile, Circe opened the scroll and read it slowly. Her mouth curved to an evil smile. She opened the jewelry box and clicked her tongue. The jewels sparkled, and she picked up one of the large pearls and looked at it closely. It was perfectly smooth and round with the color of luminous white. She placed it back into the box and closed it.

Circe's blue eyes turned to Leon and Christos, and she said, "I'll accept what King offered in exchange for my services."

"We don't know what our king asked from you," Leon replied. "If you are satisfied with the box's contents, then I guess we are ready to leave." He stood up, but as soon as he did that, Circe grabbed her wand on her belt and she waved it at Leon, who turned into a grey and white hog.

Christos stared horrified at Leon, the hog, who shrieked in terror and ran around the room.

As fast as lightning, Circe faced Christos and waved the wand toward him. He saw Circe's movements and heard her curse:

"By darkness one way

By light another.

This shall be the norm.

until your true love's heir ends your suffering. "

He didn't feel anything. He glanced at his body, still looking like an ordinary man.

Quicky, Christos ran from the room, and Circe's laughter echoed behind him, and her voice called out, "Ask your crewmate to chain you tight during the night; otherwise, your ship won't reach the land again."

Christos ran past the servant boy, who looked sad, and then past the pig pens and geese and wondered how many of those animals and birds were humans cursed to an animal form. Perhaps all of them. He ran through the forest and was out of breath when he reached the shoreline.

The goats had gone, but the small boat was there. Christos pushed it into the water and rowed back to the ship.

When he was back onboard, he told Captain Theo what he'd seen and what had happened to Leon. "He's a hog now. Circe put a spell on him. She tried to curse me too. I don't know why I didn't change to an animal."

"You look normal," Captain Theo agreed. He saw Christos hesitating and asked, "What else?"

"She said that you need to chain me at night; otherwise, this ship won't reach the land," Christos added.

Captain Theo looked distraught. "Perhaps, your curse is delayed. We'll do that as a precaution."

Christos nodded. He had no idea what the curse could be. It wasn't the same as Leon's. He turned and asked the captain, "Do you know the king's wish? What he wrote in the scroll?"

"No, I don't. He had sealed the scroll," Captain Theo replied.

"Circe said she accepted the payment for her services." Christos added, "It seemed that what Circe did to Leon was part of the service King Minos had requested for."

"Why do you believe so?" Captain Theo asked.

"Because she cursed Leon immediately after reading the scroll and cast the spell on me, too," Christos said hesitantly.

"Be careful what you say. King Minos is powerful. Don't say or do anything that would make him an enemy," Captain Theo warned Christos, who looked worried.

That's when Christos realized this trip was revenge because he had been with the queen. Someone had found out about them and told the king.

"You mentioned that you'd met Leon before this trip?" Christos asked.

"Yes, the same day when we left Crete. He came by asking about you," Captain Theo said slowly, looking as if he had put two and two together. "The king asked especially you and Leon to go to the shore to meet Circe." He put his hand on Christos's shoulder and added, "I'm sorry. I think both Leon and you were set up. You were not supposed to return from this island."

"But I did, and I will go back to Crete," Christos said with a determined look. "King Minos' plan didn't succeed."

"Let's hope you are not hexed," Captain Theo replied. "We'll sail away now from this cursed island. I don't want to be here any longer than necessary." He walked away, commanding the crew to get ready for oars, and soon the ship started moving slowly away from the island heading back to Crete. The ship cleaved the water at a steady pace, and the south wind blew, swelling the sails.

CHAPTER 9

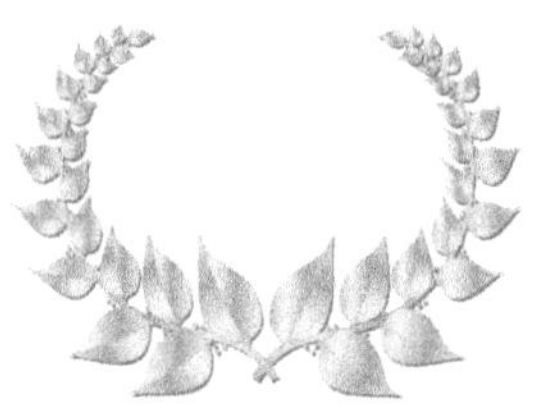

THE JOURNEY BACK TO CRETE

As the sun set on the horizon, creating pastel colors in the evening sky, the captain ordered Christos to be chained with heavy metal chains in the galley. He did not want to take any risk with Circe as he had heard rumors of her skills, and even if Christos looked to be his usual self, the captain didn't want to take any risks.

The wind picked up, and the waves had whitecaps on them as the ship pushed forward.

The night sky was dark and peppered with stars.

The first low rumbling chilled everyone on board to the bone.

"What was that?" Captain Theo asked more of himself than of his first mate and asked him to go and find out.

The second lowing sound was stronger, and now Captain Theo was sure it came from inside the ship.

Christos! the captain thought, terrified. What could have happened to the young soldier? Was it Circe's curse?

His first mate came back and said, "You have to see it yourself. You won't believe me even if I tell you."

"Take the wheel. I'll go and see myself then," Captain Theo said.

He walked along the deck with a worried look, heading to the galley where he had ordered his men to chain Christos for the night.

When he opened the door, he stood there petrified. The sight was more horrifying than he could have guessed.

He took a step back as the monster pulled his chains and lowed loudly. Christos had transformed into half a beast: he had the head of an ox, and the rest of him was human.

But he was almost twice as tall as a normal human now. His red eyes glinted evilly towards the captain, and his horns were sharp like two swords.

He couldn't speak now because the ox couldn't form words, so he mooed and lowed.

Captain Theo stared at the monstrous creature in his galley and said, "I'm sorry, Christos. I had no idea this would happen to you. This is the curse. If I interpreted it correctly, you'll be this during the night and normal during the daytime. We'll have to keep you chained every night until we reach the harbor. We can't let you lose on the ship because the beast in you would destroy the ship. That's what Circe warned you when you left her island."

Christos the Minotaur pulled his chained limbs in rage, raised his head towards the ceiling, and howled angrily. The king and the sorceress had taken his life away \ and destroyed him. He had nothing left to live for.

He recalled the curse:

"By darkness one way

By light another.

This shall be the norm.

until your true love's heir ends your suffering."

Christos wondered what the last part meant. *My true love's heir? And that person will end my suffering? That means someone will kill me.*

My true love must be Queen Pasiphaë. I love her, but she was married to King Minos. Would she have an heir with the king or with me? I don't know. I'm nothing to her now. I'm a monster. I can't love anyone, and I can't live anywhere. What will happen to me when we reach the harbor? The people will kill me or try to kill me, Christos thought, and his emotions went from anger to sadness.

His tunic and cloak had ripped to shreds when his body transformed. Only his shoes, belt, and cross belt across his chest fit now. He tied a part of his tunic as a loin cloth, so he would not be completely naked.

The ship sailed back home to Crete with the monster in their crew. Everyone on board was horrified at what Circe had done to Christo. He had been well-liked among his peers, and now he was feared.

Even in the daytime, when Christos was back to his usual self, men steered clear of him, and hardly anyone else but the captain spoke with him. He was a pariah on the ship.

Christos hated every night when his body transformed into this mutated creature with an ox's head. It was an agonizing process, and it felt like all his joints and muscles were being pulled apart. His head felt twice as large as normal, and his hearing was more acute than when he was in his human form, as was his sense of smell.

Finally, after days on the sea, the familiar shoreline with the king's palace on top of the hill was ahead of them, and the crew put all their strength into oars to get the ship back to the harbor as fast as they could.

CHAPTER 10

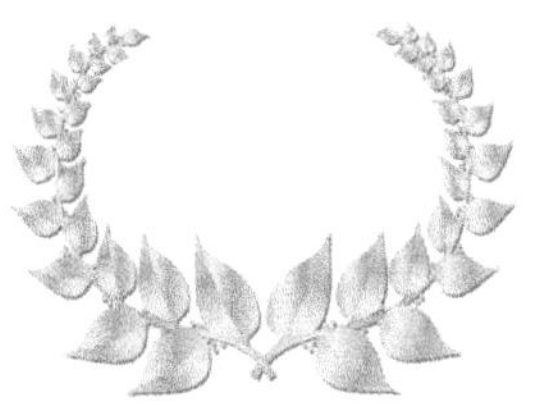

KING MINOS AND CHRISTOS

King Minos sat in his throne room, waiting impatiently for news from Circe's Island. He wanted to be sure the sorceress had done as he had asked. He stood up and paced around the room ending to face the southeast window.

The day was beautiful, with no clouds in the blue sky. The water sparkled in the sunshine, and there was hardly any wind. King Minos would have wanted a powerful wind to bring the ship back faster.

He said a quick prayer to Poseidon, the god of the waters, who was also his protector: "Please, let the winds and the waters be favorable for sailing and bring my ship back to the harbor soon." He stared at the sea, hoping to see the ship returning. He had been doing this for days now.

After five days had passed, a servant came running and announced, kneeling in front of the king, "My lord, great news. The ship you've been waiting for is back!"

King Minos stood up and took a deep breath. His heart was beating fast. He hoped that the jewelry box had been enough for Circe to do as he asked, but he wasn't sure. Circe was powerful, and she might not do as she was asked.

He recalled the scroll he had given to Captain Theo, who had no idea what was written. He had asked Circe to keep Leon and transform him into anything she would prefer. His next request was the more difficult one. He had requested a curse on Christos that would change him into a monster at night. King Minos was unsure if Circe knew how to do a curse like that, but he had heard of Circe's skills to shape humans into animals and birds. Christos's enchantment would require more skill because it would be partial shapeshifting, depending on the time of the day.

King Minos changed his clothes to more regal ones and went to the harbor with his soldiers. Wearing a white tunic with a large ox embroidery in the front, his dark blue cloak, and his jewelry crown, he marched ahead of his soldiers to the harbor.

God Poseidon had heard his wish. The ship had a strong wind from behind, heading directly to the pier where King Minos waited with his company.

"Get ready. Don't let anyone leave the ship. Everyone onboard must be imprisoned," King Minos ordered, facing his commander, lokhagos, who then told his lower-ranking officers, called ipolokhagoi, to be ready.

The king looked curiously at the crew when the ship docked on the pier. They appeared distraught but otherwise in good health. Captain Theo came ashore and kneeled in front of the king. "My king, your mission was successful. We visited the island of Circe as you had asked to." He raised his eyes to meet the king's and added, "Leon was transformed into a hog there. Christos escaped and returned home with us. However, he is not what he used to be."

"Captain Theo, thank you for your service," King Minos said and then asked, "How is Christos?"

"He is cursed. By night, he is a monster, and by day, he changes back to his human form," Captain Theo replied. He noticed that King Minos's lips curved into a wicked smile, then he turned his head to face his lokhagos. "Take the captain into a prison and capture all the crew from the ship."

"What? What is this? I did as you ordered!" Captain Theo protested as he was taken away by two soldiers. Behind him, the crew, including Christos, were captured.

As Christos passed the king, he glanced at Minos. "You knew. You gave the order to Circe because of me."

"Yes, I did," King Minos replied, smiling evilly. He told his lokhagos, "Take this man to the labyrinth and lock the gate."

"Yes, my king," the commander replied.

"The labyrinth?" Christos repeated. "It's dark there—" he started saying, and then his eyes widened as he realized that the curse was part of King Minos's revenge. He'd be imprisoned in the dark all the rest of his life as a monster because the light would never reach him and transform him back into his human form.

Defeated, he walked with the soldiers with his head down. There was nothing he could do. He'd never see his beloved queen, Pasiphaë, caress her soft skin, kiss her beautiful lips, and whisper words of love in her ear. Never would he be allowed to live his life as a human being again. Glancing upward, he saw the palace hoping that the queen would see him now for the last time as a human. She would never cast her eyes on him again because he would be a horrifying monstrous creature with no ability to speak.

The soldiers took him to the gate of the maze. It was like an opening of a cave blocked with thick iron bars. They opened the heavy lock and pushed Christos inside.

In the cave's darkness, Christos felt the shifting to a half-ox starting, and he screamed and crawled into a ball on the floor. He howled in pain as his muscles and joints spread and ripped apart, creating the monster. His head felt like someone had placed a burning iron ring around his head. After the shapeshifting was over, Christos glanced around. He saw several tunnel openings ahead of him. With his new keen sense of hearing and eyesight, he decided to go exploring.

Several tunnels led to an opening in the middle of the labyrinth, where Christos decided to stay. He knew how to return to the gate, but he'd also discovered another way out, another gate that led to a cave near the sea. When the tide was high, the water would enter the cave but not fill the whole labyrinth. He'd deduced that fact because only a part of the tunnel network was wet.

CHAPTER 11

MINOTAUR

King Minos walked down to the labyrinth gate and called out, "Christos! Come here."

A long time passed before the monstrous creature appeared from the shadows of the labyrinth.

"Ah, there you are. Let us see you in your new glory," King Minos said gleefully.

Christos stepped closer to the gate, and King Minos sighed in awe. "How clever of the witch to transform you to a part ox and part human. You know Poseidon gave me a white ox as a gift, and he favors me now." He paused and added, "Christos is not a suitable name for you now. Let's call you Minotaur." Cackling menacingly, he turned and gestured for the soldiers to come forward. They had prisoners with them. All of Christos's previous friends and colleagues were among them, including Captain Theo and his best friend, Mikhalis.

King Minos turned to face Minotaur again. "This is your meal. You will not receive anything else to eat for as long as you live. Only humans that you will kill with your own hands in your labyrinth."

If Christos could have talked, he would have been horrified, but he couldn't, and the monster in him was hungry. He had not eaten anything for days since he was taken from the ship to this maze. He stepped back, let the soldiers push the prisoners inside, and closed the gate again.

The prisoners ran away along several labyrinth passages, which only prolonged their torture. Eventually, Minotaur captured each one of them.

His first victim was Mikhalis. As he begged for mercy and to save his life, Minotaur grabbed his arm and ripped it off his body. And while alive, he ate it in front of his old friend.

Minotaur had to feed himself. That was part of the curse. As he was only one of his kind, no food was made for him, so whatever he digested was painful. During the journey on the ship, he had eaten like other humans during the daytime, but this was the first time he was a monster all the time. Now, he had to adjust his appetite to whatever was available, and that was raw human meat.

Minotaur chased all the other prisoners in the tunnels when his hunger burned inside him. Captain Theo was the last one he found. Theo had discovered the other exit from the labyrinth, but it was high tide, and the iron bars were sturdy, so he couldn't escape the horrible death. He stood there, pressing his back against the iron bars separating him from freedom and life. "Christos, I was your friend. I didn't know what King Minos had planned. Save me, please."

Minotaur pointed his sharp horns toward Theo's mid-torso and charged, impaling his body in his horns. When he shook his head, Theo took his last breath and died. Minotaur dropped the body on the tidewater, which turned crimson before floating away when the tide changed again.

Minotaur leaned against the cave wall and lowered himself to the floor. He sat there for a long time staring at Theo's dead body and the bloody water around them. He wasn't hungry after eating so many other prisoners. This body could wait. He had to save some for later as he didn't know when he would get his next meal. He was at the mercy of King Minos, and he knew it.

He raised his head to the ceiling and hollered, and his sound echoed in the cave, and it was heard in the palace and the nearby village.

Their Minotaur had taken another life.

CHAPTER 12

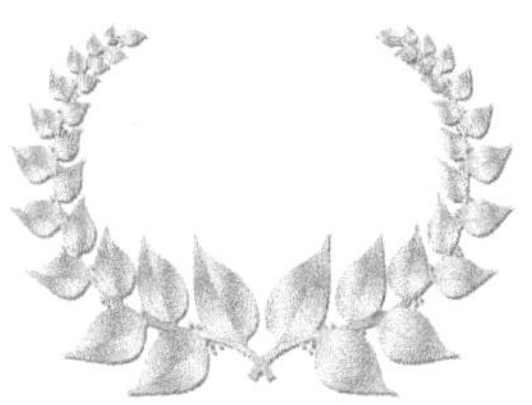

MINOTAUR AND HIS MUSE

King Minos realized that he had to feed his monster, thus, every month he had to sentence more victims to the labyrinth. Usually, King Minos sent seven prisoners to Minotaur's maze for him to kill and eat. Minotaur burned the food he ate so fast that he was always feeling hungry.

Several months went past, and then one dark night, Minotaur heard faint sounds like footsteps, rustling of clothes, and whispery voices by the other exit which led to the sea. It was not the time for the high tide, so it couldn't be any animals or birds picking the fish or other sea creatures there, he thought. His hearing was extremely acute, and he could distinguish the different sounds after living in the labyrinth for months.

"Christos!"

Minotaur's ears perked.

Someone was calling him by his human name. Who would be so foolish to come here and call him? Minotaur thought he recognized the soft voice. It sounded familiar, like the sound of the waves on a summer evening or the song of a bird. He strolled toward the other exit through the labyrinth. He didn't hurry. Whoever was there could wait. He couldn't do anything if that person was behind the gates.

As he approached the opening which was blocked with iron bars, he saw two figures standing there. The other one was a servant standing behind looking scared in the moonlight whereas the other woman was brave enough to grab the bars and she kept calling him. "Christos! Come to me, Christos."

Queen Pasiphaë saw the enormous figure approaching. She gasped, as she saw the deformed head shaped like an ox's head. The body was larger and more muscular than Christos used to have. That creature had nothing to do with Christos, she thought horrified.

When the monster was close to the bars, Pasiphaë stepped a few steps backward and said, "Christos, do you remember me?"

She pulled down the hood of her cloak and revealed her beautiful face and her long hair. She was dressed in a white gown that left her arms bare.

Minotaur heard her, but he could not talk like humans. He lowed and grabbed the bars with his hands and shook them. The metal bars were sturdy. Not even Minotaur could loosen them. King Minos had made sure of it when he closed the maze.

Queen Pasiphaë sobbed and placed her hand over her heart. "I loved you, Christos."

She gestured to the servant woman who stood behind her looking scared. "The proof of my love," she said gently.

The servant lady handed over a small bundle to Queen Pasiphaë's arms. She held the baby in her arms and smiled as she turned to Minotaur. "This is our daughter, Ariadne."

Minotaur stared at the little baby girl in her arms. And then he roared facing the moon. He realized that this baby would cause his death one day. Minotaur couldn't tell that to her because he couldn't speak. He could only utter animal-kind sounds like howling, lowing, or mooing.

Pasiphaë turned back to the servant woman and handed the baby back to her. "Wait for me by the road. I'll be there soon."

When the servant was gone, Pasiphaë returned to the iron bars. Minotaur still grabbed the bars with his human hands. The queen placed her hands over his.

Minotaur shivered. The beast inside him raged.

Queen Pasiphaë took out a mirror from his pocket and turned the mirror toward Minotaur so that the moonlight reflected directly into his eyes and face. And for a moment when the moonlight hit Minotaur, he transformed into a human. "Pasiphaë," he whispered and held out his hand touching her face gently. "I love you with all my heart."

Queen Pasiphaë leaned closer, and Christos kissed her fiercely, but when Pasiphaë closed her eyes in the kiss, her hand lowered, and the moonlight did not reflect via the mirror's surface any longer. Christos transferred into Minotaur and because Pasiphaë was in hands reach, he strangled her, and her dead body collapsed by the gate. The mirror fell off her hand onto the ground and the moonlight reflected from its shiny surface to Minotaur who temporarily changed back to a human. When he saw what he had done as a Minotaur, he fell on his knees and cried aloud grabbing and shaking the bars of his prison.

Aphrodite, the god of love and lovers, heard his heart-breaking cry and appeared by the shoreline. She took the body of the queen and brought it inside the labyrinth so that Minotaur could always have her with him there. She transformed Pasiphaë into a golden statue that looked almost alive. That was all she could do to Minotaur as Aphrodite could not or did not want to start a fight with Poseidon who was a powerful god. She knew that King Minos was under Poseidon's protection and that Minotaur was King Minos's creation.

Aphrodite faced Minotaur and said, "You know who I am."

Minotaur nodded.

"I can't give your loved one back, but I can promise you that when you die, you two will meet again. It will take years before that happens, but one day you two will be together." With those words, the god disappeared, and Minotaur was left alone in his labyrinth with the statue of his lover, his muse, keeping him company.

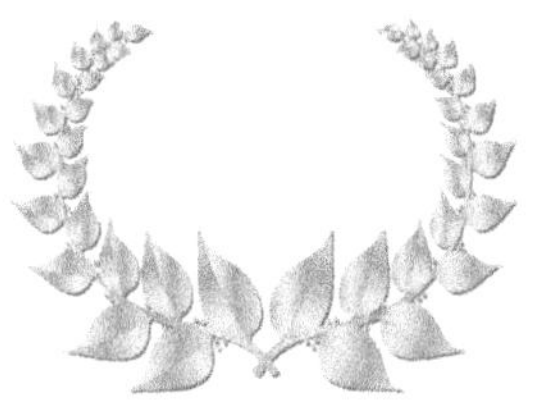

ABOUT THE AUTHOR

Meet Arla Jones, a multi-genre author hailing from the picturesque landscapes of Finland, now making waves in the literary world from the tranquil shores of Michigan. With a penchant for exploring diverse genres, the author captivates readers with tales that traverse the realms of mystery, romance, thriller, sci-fi, and fantasy, weaving intricate narratives that transport audiences to worlds both familiar and fantastical. When not penning captivating stories, the author enjoys gardening and painting.

ALSO BY THE AUTHOR

**Some of these are published as serial fiction and some
are available in different formats.**

The Starbound Orphans Series: (YA/Sci-Fi)

Starbound Orphans

Starbound Journey

The Galactic Emperor (coming soon)

The Ackley Family Saga:

Lord Ackley's Choice

A Rose So Red

Court of Kisses

Jaxon Axis -series (Dystopian, Sci-Fi):

Jaxon Axis and the First Crime

Jaxon Axis and the Ice Age

The Lost Tomb -series:

The Lost Tomb

Venemous Dunes

The Lost Oasis of Love

The Mummy Returns

Otis Thorne Thrillerseries:

Fathers and Sons

Black Dust

The Facility

Death Walks in Washington D.C.

The Ashburn -series

On Death's Door

Finders Keepers

The Kingdom Series (fantasy, romantasy, YA)

Wings of Sea

Wings of War

Wings of Shadows

Westerns

The Lady and The Stubborn Rancher

The Lady and The Robber Baron

Bury My Dreams

The Cupid and the Elf -series:

Love Trap

Naughty Elf

Ghost Stories

The Cursed Banshee

Don't Go There

Sci-Fi

The Host

Titanic Paranormal Novel

Chasing Death

Children's books:

The Attack of the Iguana

Evil Elves

The Underground Cat Academy

Bobbie Robins Contemporary thrillers:

Samantha Raven Trilogy:

I'll Be Your Shadow

I'll Never Let You Go

I'll Be Back

Ayla Jones (Dark Romance)

Donder

Bloodlines of Revolution

No Way But Down

Dragon Unleashed

Bloodlines of Revolution

Anthologies:

The Tales of Howloween

Find a full list of serial fiction, novels, and my shop: arlaj

ones.com

And also https://beacons.ai/arlajonesbooks

Tiktok: @jonesesbooks and @authorarlajones

Facebook: www.facebook.com/authorarlajones

Instagram: https://www.instagram.com/arlajonesbooks